Little Fella

Superhero

by
Sarah McConnell

 ORCHARD BOOKS

For my Mum and Dad

ORCHARD BOOKS
96 Leonard Street, London EC2A 4XD
Orchard Books Australia
14 Mars Road, Lane Cove, NSW 2066
First published in Great Britain in 2000
1 84121 623 2
Copyright © Sarah McConnell 2000
The right of Sarah McConnell to be identified as the author and
illustrator has been asserted by her in accordance with the
Copyright, Designs and Patents Act, 1988.
A CIP catalogue record for this book is available from the British Library
1 3 5 7 9 10 8 6 4 2
Printed in Singapore

Little Fella's name is Joe but everyone calls him Little Fella because he's not very big. That suits him fine most of the time, but not today ...

"Today I want to be a Superhero," said Little Fella.

"Now what do Superheroes wear?" Little Fella said.

Superheroes wear
long swirling capes.

Superheroes wear masks to
hide their faces.
And most importantly,
Superheroes wear big lace-up boots.

Is it a bird?

Is it a plane?

"You look more like a supersquirt than a Superhero," said Little Fella's Big Sister.

"Huh!" said Little Fella.
"I'll show her."
   And off went Little Fella
in search of big bad villains
who wanted to take
over the world.

It wasn't long before Little Fella found one.

"Watch out, Little Fella Superhero's about!"
shouted Little Fella, as he swirled his cape
and shooed the me-e-e-owing monster away.

Off went Little Fella to find his Big Sister.

"Look!" said Little Fella. "Look, Big Sis! I've saved a butterfly!"

"A butterfly? *That* doesn't make you a Superhero," said Little Fella's Big Sister.

But Little Fella wasn't listening. He could hear a strange noise.

"Watch out, Little Fella Superhero's about!" said
Little Fella and he pulled such a scary face that
he frightened the grrr-rowling monster away.

Off went Little Fella to find his Big Sister again. "Look," said Little Fella. "Look, Big Sis! I've rescued a ladybird." Little Fella's Big Sister rolled her eyes. "A ladybird?" she said. "*That* doesn't make you a Superhero."

Just then Little Fella heard a horrible laugh from the other side of the fence.

"Aha!" cried Little Fella. "It's the Naughty Boy from *next* door."

"Watch out, Little Fella Superhero's about!" shouted Little Fella as he stamped his big lace-up boots and frightened away the Naughty Boy.

Off went Little Fella to find his Big Sister again.

"Look," said Little Fella. "Look, Big Sis! I've saved a whole jar of snails."

"Snails? Yuck. *That* doesn't make you a Superhero," said Little Fella's Big Sister.

Little Fella's Big Sister went back inside.
"Will I *ever* be a Superhero?" said Little Fella to
the butterfly and the ladybird and the snail.
Just then Little Fella's Big Sister let out a loud cry.

"What's wrong?" shouted Little Fella
as he ran up the stairs.

"Look!" whispered Little Fella's Big Sister.

"Don't worry," said Little Fella to his Big Sister,
and to the spider, "Little Fella Superhero's here."

Little Fella gently scooped up the spider and put it on a leaf outside the window.

And this time . . .
"Little Fella," said his
Big Sister, "you really
are a Superhero!"
And she wasn't
the only one who
thought so . . .

Goodbye, Little Fella Superhero.

See you again soon!